For Ellora and Celeste - D C

LITTLE TIGER
An imprint of Little Tiger Press Limited
1 Coda Studios, 189 Munster Road, London SW6 6AW
Imported into the EEA by Penguin Random House Ireland,
Morrison Chambers, 32 Nassau Street, Dublin D02 YH68
www.littletiger.co.uk

First published in Great Britain 2025

Text copyright © Darren Chetty 2025
Illustrations copyright © Sandhya Prabhat 2025

Darren Chetty and Sandhya Prabhat have asserted their rights to be identified as the
author and illustrator of this work under the Copyright, Designs and Patents Act, 1988

A CIP catalogue record for this book is available from the British Library

Printed in China · LTP/1400/5973/1124

2 4 6 8 10 9 7 5 3 1

FSC
www.fsc.org
MIX
Paper | Supporting
responsible forestry
FSC® C104723

The Forest Stewardship Council® (FSC®) is a global, not-for-profit organisation
dedicated to the promotion of responsible forest management worldwide. FSC®
defines standards based on agreed principles for responsible forest stewardship
that are supported by environmental, social, and economic stakeholders.
To learn more, visit www.fsc.org

I'm going to make a friend

Darren Chetty   Sandhya Prabhat

LITTLE TiGER
LONDON

Hello, I'm new here.
I'm **NOT** scared.

Everyone
says I'll make
new friends . . .

but how **looong**
does it take?

Perhaps I have to wait
for them to see me.

I feel like I've been
waiting here **forever.**

I'm **really** good at making things.

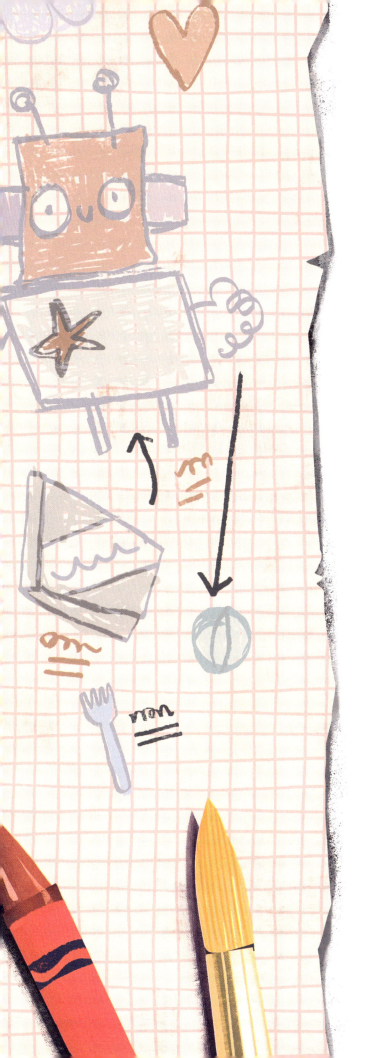

So I'm going
to make a **friend!**

What **kind** of friend

will I make?

Will my friend like **noisy fun?**

Or prefer **cosy** corners?

Will they play the games **I like**?
Or share new games?

Will they tell me lots of **stories?**

Or ask to hear mine?

Will they have **other** friends?

Or like **me** most of all?

Should they
hug me when
I'm sad?
Or give me
some **space?**

Or . . . perhaps
I can offer them
a **hug** and **ask**
if they are OK?

Together, we might be
able to put back the pieces.

And **build** and **play**, until . . .

We've **all** made a **friend!**